When I Grow Up

By Candri Hodges

Illustrated by Dot Yoder

JASON AND NORDIC PUBLISHERS
HOLLIDAYSBURG, PENNSYLVANIA

When I Grow Up

Text and illustrations copyright © 1995 Jason & Nordic Publishers

Revised art edition 2004

Library of Congress Cataloging-in-Publication Data

Hodges, Candri, 1959—

When I Grow Up / by Candri Hodges; illustrated by Dot Yoder.
 p. Cm. - - (Turtle books)
Summary: Jimmy, who is deaf, attends Career Day where he meets deaf adults with varied an interesting careers, who communicate using sign language. Includes diagrams illustrating signs for some of the words of the text.
  ISBN 0-944727-27-1. (Lib)- -ISBN 0-944727-26-3 (pbk.)
[1. Deaf- - Fiction. 2. Physically handicapped- - Fiction. 3. Occupations- -Fiction. 4. Sign Language.} I. Yoder, Dot. date– ill. II. Title. III. Series
PZ7.H6617Wh 1994
[E] - -dc20   94-6733
                                                                          CIP
                                                                          AC

ISBN 0-944727-26-3 (paper edition)
ISBN 0944727-27-1 (library binding)

Printed in the United States of America on acid free paper

To Chuck and Steven

Mom

Jimmy sat at the kitchen table watching his mother bake cookies.

"Mom," he said, signing with one hand. He had a warm oatmeal cookie in his other hand. "When you were little, did you sign or talk? Did you hear?"

"I heard and talked," Mom answered. "Why do you ask?"

"Will I hear when I grow up? Will I talk?" Jimmy asked.

Grow up

"I don't think your hearing will change," Mom signed. "And you know you have to work on your speech."

"I will be big and have hearing aids?"

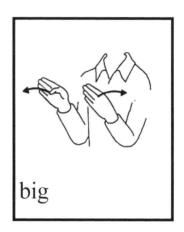

big

bus

"Yes. I know something that will help you understand. Next Tuesday we will go to school for a Career Day bus trip." Mom smiled and gave Jimmy another cookie.

Jimmy waited and waited.

At last Tuesday came and Mom an
Jimmy drove to school for that special
school bus trip.

They climbed on board a big yellow
school bus. A woman smiled at Jimmy
and gave them each a bright red name tag.
Jimmy stuck his name tag to his T-shirt.

Soon the bus was filled with boys , girls, dads and moms. A young man stood at the front of the bus.

"Hello," he said and signed.
"I hope you like our Career Day bus trip. My name is Steven. I'm your Career Day leader. Let's get started."

hello

The children laughed and played silly games as the bus rolled along. They passed houses, stores and farms.

Then the bus slowed down, slower
and slower. Up ahead, a horse and
buggy clip-clopped down the road.

An Amish girl and boy rode inside the
buggy. They stared at the bus and waved.
Mom pointed to a farmer plowing his
field. Strong horses pulled the plow.

At last they drove
through the gates of the
zoo.

"I love the zoo,"
Jimmy signed excitedly.
They all followed Steven
to the elephant park.

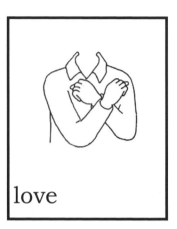

love

stink

Jimmy put his
hand over his nose. "It
stinks here," he signed.

A mother elephant and her baby
stood near a tree. Another elephant
put his trunk through the bars and
pushed Jimmy's hat off his head.

A woman stopped washing one of
the smaller elephants.

"Hello," she signed. "My name is Sarah Brenner and I'm deaf. I take care of the elephants here at City Zoo. I feed them and make their zoo home just 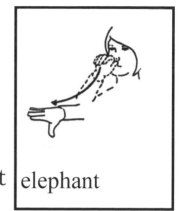 right for them to live in. Sometimes I teach them tricks, like pushing hats from boys' heads! The elephants know I'm their friend."

"Now that sounds like fun," Jimmy said.

elephant

lunch

The children were unhappy when they had to get back on the bus without seeing the rest of the zoo. Steven said, "We'll come back another day, but we have two more stops before lunch."

Soon the bus stopped in front of a school.

"This school is different," Jimmy signed when they went inside. The tables were covered with all kinds of paints, pencils and paper.

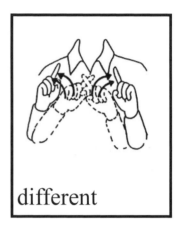

different

"My name is Patty Brown and I'm deaf," a young woman signed. "This is an art school."

She picked up a ball of clay and began to make something with it.

school

Patty pushed and rolled the clay. Soon she showed them a rabbit with long ears and a round tail.

"I like that," Mom signed.

Next the bus stopped at WALKER'S LAWN CARE. Jimmy could see green trees, bushes and many bright colored flowers inside and outside the little store.

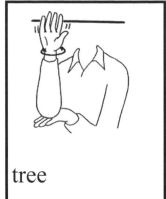

tree

A man with hearing aids met them. "My name is Michael Walker. I like to work with plants and I like to be outdoors, so I opened my own lawn care store," Mr. Walker signed.

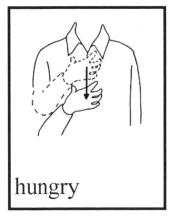

hungry

They thanked Mr. Walker and climbed back on the bus.

"I'm hungry," Jimmy signed.

"Our next stop is lunch," Steven answered.

At the restaurant a man with red hair and a white apron met them.

He waved a spoon in the air. "My name is Daniel, "the man signed. "I am deaf. My father asked me to tell you that he is also deaf. He is a teacher."

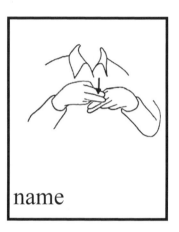

name

food

"Now I'm going to make your food."
"I want a cheese-burger and french fries, please," Jimmy signed.

After lunch they met
a young man who worked
in a factory making boats.

"Hello, my name is
Peter and I'm deaf," he
signed. "I like to go
sailing, so I think working
with boats is as much fun
as playing with them." He smiled.
"Almost."

like

I

They said goodbye to
Peter and went to the
factory office. They met a
woman working at a
computer.

"Hi, my name is Ann.
I'm doing a new
computer program for
the factory," she signed.
"I also am deaf."

Outside the factory they met a twelve year old boy just starting out with his bag full of newspapers.

"This is my friend, John," Steven signed. "He brings my paper everyday. John is deaf."

"I like delivering papers and meeting all my neighbors," John signed.

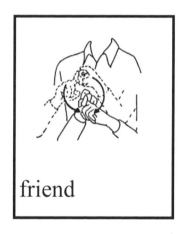

friend

The children were quiet on the way back to school. "Everyone was a different age and everyone had a different job," Jimmy thought as he looked out the bus window.

"How did you like Career Day?" Dad asked that night as they ate dinner.

"I liked it a lot," Jimmy said. "And do you know what I'm going to be when I grow up?"

day

grow up

Dad and Mom looked at Jimmy, waiting for him to answer his own question.

"When I grow up I'm going to be deaf and..."

"...anything I want to be."

DICTIONARY

big
B shape both hands, palms facing, tips out. Move away from one another.

bus
B shape both hands, left palm right, right palm left. Place little finger side of right B against left index then draw RH back toward body.

cheese
Twist heel of right palm on heel of left palm.

day
Hold left arm before you palm down, tips right. Point right index finger up. Then rest right elbow on back of left hand and arc down to elbow.

different
Cross index fingers and pull apart so that fingers point outward. Repeat.

elephant
Place back of right curved open B on nose and trace trunk of elephant downward.

flower
RH flat O. Place tips on right side of nose then arc to left side.

food
Place tips of flat O on mouth.

friend
Hook right X over left X which is turned up, then reverse.

grow, raise, grown

hamburger
Clasp hands together, reverse position and clasp together again, as if forming a patty.

hello
Place index tip of H shape RH at side of forehead then move out.

31

hungry
Draw tips of claw hand down upper chest.

I
I shape RH palm left. Place thumb side on chest.

like (verb)
Place right middle finger and thumb on upper chest, then draw out and close fingers.

love
S shape both hands. Cross wrists and place over heart.

lunch (alt.)
Index tip of right L, palm in, rotates in small circle in front of mouth.

mommy (mamma)
Five shape RH palm left, tips up. Tap chin with thumb twice.

name
H shape both hands, left palm right, palm in. Hit left H with right H.

school
Open B both hands, left palm up, tips out; right palm down, tips left. Clap hands twice.

stink
Hold nose with thumb and index finger of RH.

tree
Five shape RH palm left. Place right elbow on back of LH and shake RH rapidly.

up
Point index finger up.

want
Five shape both hands, palms up, fingers slightly curved. Draw back to body.